Adapted by Alice Alfonsi

Based on the television series, "That's So Raven", created by Michael Poryes and Susan Sherman

Part One is based on the episode written by Sarah Jane Cunningham & Suzie V. Freeman

Part Two is based on the episode written by Dava Savel

New York

Printed in the United States of America

First Edition
1 3 5 7 9 10 8 6 4 2

Library of Congress Control Number: 2005921767

ISBN 0-7868-3600-8

For more Disney Press fun, visit www.disneybooks.com
Visit DisneyChannel.com

Part One

Chapter One

I can't believe it, thought Raven Baxter, my dad's restaurant is going to open in less than a week.

Standing beside her two best friends, Raven grinned as her father flipped the switch on the restaurant's cool new neon sign. THE CHILL GRILL glowed blue against the dining room's front wall. Everyone hooted and clapped.

"Congratulations!" cried Raven's mother. She threw her arms around her husband. "Baby, this restaurant is everything we ever dreamed of."

"Oh, yeah!" Raven agreed. She was especially proud of the decor. Her dad wanted the place to be a hit with the "younger crowd," so he'd put Raven in charge of interior design. If there was one thing Raven *loved* to do, it was take charge! Plus, her fashion design skills had come in really handy when she was picking out colors.

She'd chosen a sunny yellow color for the brick walls, pale blue for the floors and chairs, and dusty rose for the tables. The combination made the large space feel warm and welcoming, yet bright and festive, too. A retro jukebox and splashes of colorful graffiti added to the overall fly factor.

"Way to go, Mr. Baxter!" cried Raven's good friend, Chelsea Daniels.

"This place is the bomb!" added Eddie Thomas, Raven's other homey.

"And the best part is, this is *my* place," Mr. Baxter proudly replied. "I mean, finally, *I'm* the boss and nobody can tell me what to do."

"Yeah, that's sweet," said Raven, picking up

a box of plump California tomatoes. This whole turn-on-the-sign party is cute and all, she thought, but the Grill isn't even close to being ready for customers. What this place needs is fewer props and more prep! "Hey, Dad?" she said, shoving the box of tomatoes into her father's arms. "Get back to work."

"Uh, Rae," said Mr. Baxter. "I know you're excited about the opening and all, but let me explain to you how it works at The Chill Grill. *I* grill, *you* chill." With that, Mr. Baxter shoved the tomatoes right back at his daughter and pointed to the kitchen door.

As Mr. Baxter walked away, Raven dropped the box back onto the tabletop. *What* is my dad thinking? she wondered. I've got to plan opening night. I can't be bothered with *produce*. . . . Now where are Chelsea and Eddie? she wondered, glancing around the room. I've got jobs for them.

Raven spotted her two best friends filling empty napkin dispensers. She was about to cross the room and give them their "to do" lists when she heard someone tapping a microphone. Raven looked up at the restaurant's small stage to find her mother standing there.

"Test one, two." Mrs. Baxter's voice echoed off the dining room's yellow brick walls. "Shoo doo . . . Shoo dooby doo . . . Shoo doo duh doo dwee-bop! Shimmy shimmy!"

Oh, snap! Raven thought. *What* are those messed-up sounds coming out of my mother's mouth?

Raven rushed over to the stage. "Mom. Mom, what are you doing?" she cried.

Mrs. Baxter stared at her freaked-out daughter. "I'm scattin'," she informed her calmly. "Scoot didilly-oot scoot!"

Raven vaguely remembered something about scattin'. It was some sort of jazz thing—

what folks did back in the day. But *old* school isn't going to fly with kids from *my* school, she thought.

"That's cute," Raven told her mom, "but what if someone actually heard you?" She shook her head. "No way. I mean, you know, there's going to be a lot of kids from school hanging around The Chill Grill."

Mrs. Baxter put a hand on her hip. "'Scuse you," she snapped. "I'm just doing a sound check. You know, we're going to have live entertainment opening night."

"We are?!" Raven was outraged. I *cannot* believe I was left out of the loop, she thought. "Mom, when was this decided?"

Before Mrs. Baxter could reply, her daughter climbed onto the restaurant stage.

"'Scuse me," Raven announced impatiently, grabbing the mike from her mother. "People, people, people, listen up, people!"

From the dining room floor, Raven's father and her little brother, Cory, glanced up. Across the room, Eddie and Chelsea looked up, too.

"Okay," Raven continued. "This place has to be cool because . . . as we all know, it is a reflection upon *me*."

Mr. Baxter folded his arms and narrowed his eyes.

"So the following things are uncool: Mom scatting. Yeah, that's got to go. Two . . . Dad's face on these flyers." Raven held up a Chill Grill flyer with her father's face on it to prove her point. I love my dad, she thought, but his goofy mug is not gonna bring the kids in! "Got to go!" she proclaimed.

From the dining room floor, Cory looked at the big box of tomatoes and selected the one that'd be best to throw at his annoying sister. He found a nice big one and grabbed it.

Cory gave the tomato a kiss, then tossed it

up and down like a baseball. "Just say the word, Dad," he whispered.

"Number three . . . Cory," Raven continued from the stage. She didn't bother announcing a ban on anything her little brother might do. It was bad enough he was even hanging around the restaurant. "Got to go!"

Okay, that does it, thought Cory, taking aim.

"Know what?" added Raven. "Actually, make Cory number *one*. So, starting over from the top. Number one . . ."

Across the room, Eddie turned to Chelsea and jerked his thumb at the stage. "Man," he whispered. "Raven's really trippin' over this restaurant thing."

"Yeah, I know," said Chelsea, shaking her head. "She has to control everything."

"Which is exactly why we can't tell her what we're doing," Eddie reminded her.

Just then, a loud *splat*! came from the stage. Eddie and Chelsea looked up to find Raven glaring at her little brother. The remains of a smashed tomato were dripping from her stylin', white, hand-embroidered jacket.

Cory smiled at his sister and shrugged. "It slipped?" he tried.

"My *foot* is going to *slip*!" Raven shouted as she tore off her new high-heeled mules.

Cory's eyes widened as his sister took off her shoes. If there was one thing he'd learned, it was this: when the high heels came off, Raven meant business.

Dang, he thought, she might actually catch me this time! A second later, he was off and running.

"Get back here, Cory!" cried Raven, as she chased after him.

Mr. Baxter threw up his hands when he saw his kids racing around his new restaurant. "If you kids break anything!" he cried, taking off after them. "Stop it! I mean it. Both of you!"

"Victor, *you* stop," cried Mrs. Baxter, "you're going to sprain something! You always do!" Then she ran after Mr. Baxter.

Eddie and Chelsea stared dumbfounded at the Baxter family. Raven was chasing Cory, Mr. Baxter was chasing Raven, and Mrs. Baxter was chasing Mr. Baxter.

Man, thought Eddie, this is one wack conga line. He caught Chelsea's eye and pointed at the nearest door. She nodded enthusiastically.

"Anyway," Eddie called to the Baxters as he inched toward the exit. "Y'all have fun."

"Yeah," added Chelsea, joining him. "You know what? We're just going to see ourselves out. Thanks!"

Chapter Two

When Raven's dad was looking for a place to open his restaurant, he had said location was the most important thing. So with props to her father, Raven picked the hottest location at school to pass out flyers for the restaurant— right in front of the trophy display case.

It's perfect, Raven decided. Tons of kids pass by here. Plus, the trophies represent determination, achievement, and excellence. Add *outstanding* burgers and onion rings, and you've got The Chill Grill!

Raven was there with a handful of flyers during every break between classes. She wouldn't let *anyone* walk by her without giving them one.

"Come to the grand opening of The Chill

Grill!" she cried. "Cool food, cool people, cool bathrooms—well, they're not really that cool, just superclean. But I guess you can say that's cool. Right?"

Raven knew she was pouring it on a little thick. But she believed in her dad's dream. Besides, she thought, a restaurant in my family makes *me* supercool. Well, even more super-cool than I already am.

Raven turned to hand out yet another flyer and spotted Devon Carter. Yum, she thought.

She ran to catch up with him. "Hey, Devon. Hey, how're you doin'?"

Devon turned. "Hey, what's up, Raven?"

Raven gazed into his chocolate brown eyes. "Did I give you one of these?"

"Only a hundred." Devon reached into his backpack and pulled out a whole stack of Chill Grill flyers. "But I could always use another one," he added politely.

Dang, she thought, the boy is sweeter than honey! Raven placed yet another flyer in his hand.

Devon smiled when he saw Raven's face on the advertisement. "That's a cute picture," he said.

Raven beamed. Devon thinks I look cute, C-U-T-E, cute, she thought to herself. "Thanks, it was my dad's idea," she lied. But it was only a small fib. He had agreed to the new look for the flyer . . . once she suggested it! "So, Devon, do you think you can make it?" she asked.

Devon thought about it for a moment. "Are you going to have egg rolls?"

Raven leaned close to let her boy in on a little secret. "It's not a Chinese restaurant."

Devon frowned. "That's too bad. It's, like, all I eat." Then he turned and headed down the hall.

Oh, no, you don't! Raven thought as she

desperately chased after him. "Wait, Wait. Devon, Devon. Get back here," she cried, tugging on his sleeve.

Devon stopped. Raven banged the side of her head like she was clearing her ears after a swim in the ocean. "I don't think I heard you correctly! Did you say, *egg* rolls? Of course we've got egg rolls. We're rollin' with the egg rolls. You better stop me, I'm on the egg roll!"

"Cool," Devon said with a smile. "I'll try to make it."

Raven's heart fluttered as she watched him stride off to his next class. "Okay, bye, Devon-derfulicious-ness," she said with a sigh.

Raven wanted to tell her homeys the great news. Luckily, she didn't have to go very far to find them. Eddie and Chelsea were just across the hall, standing by their lockers. Their heads were together and they were talking quietly, ignoring everyone else.

Raven hurried over. As she got close, Eddie and Chelsea stopped talking.

"Guys! Major news," Raven squealed. "Devon Carter is going to try to come to opening night. Do you know what that means?"

Eddie frowned.

Chelsea rolled her eyes. "Yeah," she groaned. "More work for us."

"Exactly," Raven replied. "Chelsea, I'm going to need a wardrobe conference, and Eddie, I'm going to need egg roll recipes."

Eddie shrugged. "Okay. But what if we have other plans?"

Had she heard Eddie right? Had he said something crazy about "having other plans"?

Raven giggled. "Please . . . *plans*? That I don't *know* about? That is pretty hilarious."

Eddie and Chelsea exchanged glances, and laughed politely with their best friend. Then

Eddie stopped laughing. "But seriously, Rae. We *do* have other plans," he told her.

Raven was amazed—and a little bit hurt, too. How could they have plans that don't involve *me*, she thought. Aren't we tight?

"What are y'all doing?" Raven asked. She tried not to sound disappointed.

"Bowling," said Eddie.

"Surfing," cried Chelsea at the same time.

Raven's eyes narrowed suspiciously. She shot her friends a doubtful look, so they tried again.

"Surfing," Eddie declared.

"Bowling," Chelsea insisted.

Now Raven was *really* suspicious.

"Actually, we're bowling and surfing," Eddie explained. Chelsea nodded.

"Yeah, right, right," Chelsea said. "We're *blurfing*."

Raven blinked. "Blurfing?" Is that a word? she asked herself.

"Yeah," said Eddie, trying to sound convincing. "See, you bowl on a surfboard. And it's cool, except for . . ." He shrugged. "You know . . . the board scratches the lanes. 'Cause they're still working out the kinks and stuff."

Frowning, Raven stared at her friends. Did they really expect her to believe them? "So, y'all can't help out 'cause you've got to go blurf?"

"Yeah, Rae. Sorry," said Chelsea. "But it's not up to *us*. We're in a league."

Chelsea touched Eddie's arm. "We better go," she said. They hurried off together.

A confused Raven watched them go. Okay, she thought, something is *definitely* up with Eddie and Chelsea. And I am *definitely* going to find out what it is!

Chapter Three

When Raven got up and went downstairs the next morning, her dad was busy cooking breakfast. Her mother was getting fruit out of the fridge. And her brother was sitting at the table, his plate already clean.

Pots clanged and the skillet sizzled, but Raven didn't have much of an appetite. What little she'd had in the first place quickly vanished when she saw her brother's new "friend."

"What's that?!" Raven cried, gaping in horror at the hideous ventriloquist dummy.

Mrs. Baxter put a protective arm around Cory, her grin as plastic as the flowers at the dentist's office. "This is Monty," Mrs. Baxter said. "Isn't he cute and *not creepy* at all?"

Monty the Dummy had wiry brown hair, bulging blue eyes, and a sinister smile that showed too many teeth. His outfit wasn't much better. He wore a tacky black tuxedo jacket, bow tie, and orange pants.

"Cory is working on a ventriloquist act for opening night," Mr. Baxter called from over by the stove.

Raven stared at the dummy on Cory's lap. "What's the act?" she asked, although part of her was afraid to hear the answer.

"Hey, toots," said Cory, speaking through the dummy. "Halloween's over, you can take off that mask now. What's up with *thaaaat?*"

Raven shuddered. She didn't know what was worse—the lame joke or the bizarre clicking mouth of the wooden-headed doll. *Dang,* she thought, it's bad enough Eddie and Chelsea don't want to kick it with me anymore. Now I have to eat breakfast with a dummy—and a creepy-looking doll.

Raven sighed at Cory. "Okay, dummy and dumber, I've got to go."

Mrs. Baxter turned to her son. "Come on, Cory. Time for school."

Cory jumped out of his chair. "Monty, too?" he asked.

Mrs. Baxter sighed. "Fine, but *he* rides in the trunk."

"What's up with *thaaaat?*" yelled Monty.

Raven was glad to see her brother go. She sat down at the table across from her father, who had finished cooking.

"Hey, Dad, I have a question—"

"Rae," he cut in, already knowing what was coming. "I told you, I'm *not* putting egg rolls on the menu."

"Oh, come on, Dad," Raven argued. "Egg rolls are sweeping the nation. Four out of five kids surveyed said when it comes to rolls, *egg* is their favorite . . . uh . . . followed by cinnamon and Tootsie."

Mr. Baxter just shook his head. "Rae, forget about egg rolls. If you really want to help, why don't you, Eddie, and Chelsea come down to The Chill Grill after school and help set the tables?"

Raven sighed. "They can't," she said.

Mr. Baxter was surprised. "Why not?"

"Because they've got to *blurf*," huffed Raven.

Mr. Baxter scratched his head. "Say what?"

But before Raven could explain, she suddenly felt dizzy. The whole kitchen began to spin, and in a flash, she found herself in the midst of one of her psychic visions.

Through her eye
The vision runs
Flash of future
Here it comes—

Okay, please tell me what I'm looking at? Why is everything so small? Oh, I get it! I'm looking through a peephole. I wonder why?

Omigosh, it's Eddie and Chelsea. They're standing alone in a living room. Eddie is pulling Chelsea close. They're locking eyes and putting their arms around each other!

Oh, no! I am not seeing this! What's coming next—a kiss? Show me, vision, show me!

Raven blinked. She was suddenly back in her kitchen, clutching the table to steady herself.

"Well!" she exclaimed. "*Now* I know what *blurfing* is."

Mr. Baxter's eyes widened. He knew his daughter had just had a vision. "What did you see?" he asked worriedly.

"It's a disaster," Raven moaned. "Eddie and

Chelsea, they looked like they were about to . . . to . . . *kiss*!"

Mr. Baxter smiled with relief. "So? Why is that so bad?" he asked.

Raven rolled her eyes at her totally clueless father. "Because Dad, we've always been a threesome," Raven replied. "If they become a *twosome*, then I become a *onesome*. Then if they break up, we become three onesomes, which is definitely not as good as one threesome."

Mr. Baxter's head was spinning. Onesomes? Twosomes? He was lost. "Rae. Sometimes your visions aren't exactly what you think they are," he reminded her.

Raven shook her head. I know what I saw, she told herself. So why is my dad trying to spin it?

"Look, Rae," Mr. Baxter continued. "Why don't you just ask Eddie and Chelsea straight up what's going on?"

Raven nodded. That is the best advice my dad has given me all week!

"Yeah," she told him, "I guess you're right."

Later at school, Raven spotted Chelsea and Eddie huddling together next to the trophy case. They stopped talking as soon as they saw Raven. Chelsea tried to go one way and Eddie tried to go the other way. Somehow Raven managed to corner both of them.

"Hey," said Raven. "So, what's going on with you two?"

"Nothing," Eddie and Chelsea said.

Well, at least this time they got their answers straight, thought Raven. At least they weren't trying to give her another lame story about *blurfing*.

"Oh," said Raven suspiciously. "'Cause lately it kinda seems like *something*."

Chelsea quickly shook her head. "Well, uh,

sometimes nothing can *seem* like something," she replied.

Raven's eyes narrowed. "And yet sometimes, something can actually *be* something," she said.

"Unless it's *nothin'*," Eddie said.

Raven stared at her friends. "Nothing *yet*? Or nothing at all? 'Cause if it's nothing at all, we can do it *together*."

Eddie shook his head. "Can't," he told her.

Raven tossed her hair. "Why not?"

"Because," said Chelsea. "If three people do nothing, then it actually becomes *something*."

The school bell rang, and Eddie and Chelsea hurried off to class. Raven chased after them, more certain than ever that her two best friends had something going on.

Chapter Four

As Raven walked into health class her eyes went wide. Her teacher's desk looked like a junkyard hit by a tornado. The only thing nastier than the mess on Mr. Grozowtski's desk was the horrible green sweater he was wearing.

Raven decided that the next time her health teacher cleaned out his desk, he should post a warning sign—something like BEWARE! TOXIC WASTE DUMP!

Everyone took their seats as Mr. Grozowtski rummaged through the papers, folders, office supplies, and unidentifiable debris piled high on his desk.

"Hey, Mr. Grozowtski," said Eddie. "Are

we ever going to get our reports back?"

Mr. Grozowtski made a sour face. "About your reports . . . For some reason, I'm having a little trouble locating them."

The whole class groaned. Not again!

"All right, all right, all right, that's enough already," grumbled Mr. Grozowtski. He held up their textbook. "Just read the next chapter in *At Least You Have Your Health*. I'll search through my desk."

Everyone opened their books while Mr. Grozowtski rummaged through his mess. Raven looked around and noticed that Chelsea was writing a note on pink stationery. When she finished, she folded the note and tossed it to Eddie, who was sitting a few seats behind her.

What have we here? Raven wondered. A little love note, perhaps?

Raven watched as Eddie read the note and

smiled. Then he scribbled something on the pink paper and tossed it back to Chelsea. But Chelsea was facing forward, so she didn't see him toss it. And Eddie hadn't seemed to notice that his throw was short. The paper had landed on the floor, just a few feet from Raven's desk.

"Come to mama," Raven whispered. She reached out with the pointy toe of her new suede boots. Just as she was about to snag the note, a giant loafer smashed down on the delicate pink paper.

"It's mine now," snarled Mr. Grozowtski.

Raven groaned silently. Okay, minor setback.

Mr. Grozowtski picked up the note and walked back to his desk. He dropped the note into the trash can and sank back into his chair. If I don't clean out my desk I'll never find those reports, he thought to himself.

Across the room, Raven thought fast. She took out her pencil and snapped the point against the edge of the desk. Then she jumped up and went to the front of the classroom. Mr. Grozowtski looked up.

"Hi," said Raven timidly. "I just want to, you know, sharpen my pencil." *And* get that note, she thought.

"No!" growled Mr. Grozowtski.

Raven jumped, startled. Then her teacher chuckled. "I'm kidding. Go ahead."

Raven went to the supply desk and shoved the pencil into the sharpener. Meanwhile, Mr. Grozowtski reached into his desk and pulled out a greasy old lunch bag. He opened it and peeked inside. The stink of rotten fruit made him crinkle his nose.

Whoa. How old is this? Mr. Grozowtski said to himself, pulling out a black-and-brown banana.

Raven was about to reach into the wastebasket when Mr. Grozowtski dropped the nasty-looking banana into the trash. Raven yanked her hand back and pretended to sharpen her pencil. Totally grossed out, she watched Mr. Grozowtski take something green and fuzzy out of the greasy paper bag.

Mr. Grozowtski studied the object in his hand, wondering just what it was. A guacamole sandwich? he asked himself. Then Mr. Grozowtski snapped his fingers. I remember, he thought, that was *chicken salad*!

Holding his nose, Mr. Grozowtski tossed the sandwich into the trash. He opened another drawer and pulled out a pair of socks.

I used to love these old sweat socks, Mr. Grozowtski thought. Hey, there's still some sweat in them.

Raven sharpened her pencil and watched while Mr. Grozowtski wrung the socks out over the wastebasket. Finally, he tossed in the old socks.

Raven was getting more grossed out by the second. The worst part was she could see the pink paper peeking out from under the rotten banana, green moldy sandwich, and sweat socks. Still, Raven was determined to read that note, no matter what.

Mr. Grozowtski opened another drawer in his desk. This is fun, he thought. I wonder what else is in here?

He pulled out an old carton of milk, shook it, then checked the date stamped on the side.

Hmmm, expires April fifteenth, he thought. Mr. Grozowtski's eyes bugged when he saw the year. 1993!?! Whoa, whoa, whoa!

Mr. Grozowtski quickly dumped the sour milk into the trash. It was so old and foul, it came out of the carton in foul-smelling chunks.

Mr. Grozowtski struggled to open the next drawer, which was stuck. Come on, come on, he grunted. Suddenly, the drawer flew open. It was filled with student papers.

Mr. Grozowtski frowned. Oh, nuts. I found the reports, he thought. *Now* I have to grade them. Irritated, he looked out at the class. "Does anybody have a pencil?" Mr. Grozowtski asked.

Raven yanked her pencil out of the sharpener. She'd been sharpening the pencil for so long that there wasn't much left. She rushed over to her teacher's desk and handed it to him. Pinching the little pencil between his meaty fingers, Mr. Grozowtski began to grade the papers.

Before she returned to her seat, Raven stooped down. Very carefully, so the teacher wouldn't notice, she picked up the small wastebasket and carried it back to her seat with her. A nasty smell rose from the garbage, but she ignored it. Raven knew what she had to do. Taking a deep breath and holding it, Raven prepared herself to be grossed out, big-time.

Here you go, she thought, and reached into the garbage. She felt around in the muck. *Ew, ew, ew . . . !*

Finally, her fingers closed around the love note and she slowly pulled her hand out. Raven nearly hurled when she saw the globs of messy, smelly, super-gross gunk stuck to her arm, all the way up to her elbow.

Ew, ew, ew, ew, ew!

Trying hard not to throw up, Raven held the yucky note away from her face as she unfolded it carefully. Raven recognized Chelsea's handwriting immediately.

"Eddie," Chelsea wrote. "Must meet at my house after school. Sink broken, have to wait for plumber."

Interesting, thought Raven. Then she looked for Eddie's answer. "I'll be there," he wrote back.

I knew it! Raven told herself. They *do* have something going on. I've got to put a stop to this. Then she remembered the toxic waste on her arm. Right *after* I take a three-hour shower, she thought.

Chapter Five

Eddie and Chelsea faced each other in the middle of Chelsea's living room. Arms outstretched, their hands met. With fingers entwined, Chelsea took a deep breath.

"Are you ready?" Eddie asked softly.

"Yes," whispered Chelsea. Then she lowered her hands and stomped her foot. "No! I'm sorry," she cried. "I just can't stop thinking about how we're sneaking behind Raven's back."

"Chels, you know Rae," Eddie said. "I mean, if she knew that we were practicing a dance for her dad's opening night, she'd wind up trying to control the whole thing."

Chelsea nodded. "Yeah, she'd probably want us to do everything *her* way."

"It's better to just leave her clueless," Eddie said, shrugging.

Chelsea nodded in agreement. "You know, it's always worked for me. Ready?"

Eddie reached out and took Chelsea in his arms. But before they could make their first move, there was a knock at the door.

Chelsea broke away. "Oh, I'm sorry. That must be our plumber."

Chelsea opened the door to find the weirdest-looking plumber she'd ever seen.

"Hello," said Chelsea.

"Hey there, little lady," rumbled a gruff, low voice. "I'm your plumber." Then Raven lumbered into the living room, but she didn't look at all like herself. She wore blue overalls stuffed with pillows to make her body look as wide as it was tall. Around her pillowed-up waist she sported a heavy tool belt. A baseball cap covered her wild, frizzy wig. On top of a fake nose, Raven wore tiny, round glasses that hid her eyes. Under it she wore a dark fake mustache. Her dad's shoe polish, carefully applied, created the "manly," unshaven look. A red metal toolbox, and a four-foot hand drill completed Raven's disguise.

"You all just keep on doin' what you're doin'. I'm called the *invisible plumber*. So I'm just going to be invisible," growled Raven as she moved toward the bathroom door.

"Oh, actually, sir. It's our *upstairs* bathroom," Chelsea informed who she *thought* was the plumber.

"Hey, little lady," Raven barked loudly. "*Who* is your plumber?"

Chelsea blinked and stepped back. "You are," she said nervously.

"So what's my name?" Raven asked.

Chelsea stood at attention. "Mr. Plumber, sir!"

Raven crossed to the bathroom. When she

passed by Eddie, she quickly turned her face away, worried he might recognize her.

Inside the bathroom, Raven pretended to examine the sink. But she was mainly stealing peeks at Eddie and Chelsea through the open door.

"Okay, so where were we?" Eddie said, taking Chelsea's hand.

"Oh, hang on a second. I'm going to go put on our song," said Chelsea.

"They have a song," Raven gasped. She dropped the toolbox with a crash.

Chelsea heard the noise and crossed to the bathroom. "Actually, I'm sorry, sir," she said. "We could use a little bit of privacy." Chelsea closed the door in Mr. Plumber's face.

Then she returned to the living room, started the music, and took Eddie by the hand.

"Okay," Eddie said. "Now we can get our groove on!"

Raven overheard and was shocked. "They have a groove?" she said.

"All right, let's do it," said Chelsea. "No more interruptions."

Raven couldn't believe what she was hearing. She needed to see it with her own eyes. But the door was closed now. Thinking fast, Raven took the hand drill from her toolbox and drilled a peephole in the bathroom wall.

When Raven looked through it, she saw Eddie and Chelsea locked in an embrace.

Raven chewed the end of her fake mustache. "Just like my vision!" she groaned.

Chelsea looked around. "You know what?" she said. "We need more room."

With Eddie's help, Chelsea pushed a chair to the wall, blocking Raven's peephole. Raven frantically grabbed the hand drill again and drilled a hole right through the back of the chair.

"It's getting a little hot in here," Eddie

declared. "Let me take this off real quick." Eddie took off his jacket and threw it over the chair.

Once again, Raven's view was blocked. She picked up the drill, pushed it through the peephole, and began to drill once more. Eddie would never notice a little hole in his jacket.

"Okay, ready," said Eddie. He embraced Chelsea. "That's it, Chels. Just relax in my arms."

Raven heard Eddie's words and drilled even faster. But the jacket got caught on the end of her drill.

Standing in the living room, Chelsea saw the jacket wiggle and jump and twirl around and around. "Uh, Eddie," she said, backing away from the crazy dancing jacket. "I think your jacket's alive!"

Eddie couldn't believe his eyes. "What in the world?"

Chelsea ran to the bathroom door and knocked. "Excuse me? Hello?" she called. "Is everything all right?"

Startled, Raven yanked the drill out of the wall and fell backward, over the toolbox. The drill clattered to the floor with a terrible racket.

As Chelsea threw open the bathroom door, Raven dove under the sink. "I was just wondering if everything is all right in here?" Chelsea asked.

From under the sink, Raven nodded. "Yes. No worries." She tapped a pipe with her wrench. "Now I'm a plumber, so I'm plumbin'. 'Cause that's what plumbers do. Now get out!"

"Okay then," Chelsea left and closed the door behind her.

Raven decided she'd better go. But when she stood up, her bracelet fell off her wrist and slipped down the drain.

"My bracelet!" she cried. "Omigosh! Oh, no!"

Raven grabbed a wrench and dove back under the sink. She saw a big nut on the bottom of the drainpipe. "I wonder what this does?"

Raven twisted the nut and a jet of water hit her face. "And now I know."

Raven removed a piece of pipe and stuck her hand inside. "Okay. Come on. That's my favorite bracelet. Come on. Get out of there. Aha! Got it!"

In the living room, the doorbell rang.

"Who is it?" Chelsea called.

"Plumber!" called a voice from the other side of the front door.

Chelsea answered the door, surprised. "Hi, come in," she said. "I didn't realize this was a *two*-plumber job."

From inside the bathroom, Raven heard the

other plumber arrive—and she panicked. A few seconds later, she was racing across the living room.

"Hey there," she called to the other plumber as she hurried toward the front door.

She wanted to get away clean—without the man asking *why* her hand was stuck in a drainpipe. So she made up a reason fast.

"Make sure you've got one of these in your kit," she advised, raising her pipe-covered hand. "Plumbers salute!"

And then she was gone.

Chapter Six

It was opening night at The Chill Grill, and the place was jumping. Families and teens, most of them Raven's classmates, filled the tables and booths.

At the door, Raven was playing hostess. As folks streamed inside she handed out menus.

When the time looked right, Mrs. Baxter hopped onto a low stage built under the blue neon Chill Grill sign. She picked up the microphone and addressed the crowd. "Welcome to The Chill Grill!" she began. "How's everybody doing?"

Cheers and applause filled the dining room.

"Thank you," said Mrs. Baxter. "Now our

first act is two very funny guys. Please put your hands together for the comedy stylings of Cory Baxter and his pal, Monty!"

Cory actually looked pretty good in a pressed shirt and sharply knotted tie, not that Raven would ever tell him that. He stepped onto the stage, his dummy, Monty, resting on his arm.

"Thank you. Thank you," said Cory. Then he looked at his dummy. "Hey, Monty, what did you think of my dad's oatmeal he cooked this morning?"

"I'll let you know when I get done chewing it," said Monty. "What's up with *thaaat*?"

The audience laughed and clapped. Mr. Baxter forced a polite chuckle, then turned to Mrs. Baxter and frowned. "My oatmeal's not chewy," he hissed. "That dummy's gonna be firewood."

Mrs. Baxter touched her husband's arm.

"Now, Victor, chill," she told him. "Cory's just poking a little fun at you."

"And what about my mom?" Cory continued on the stage. "Isn't she pretty?"

In the audience, Mrs. Baxter smiled.

"Yeah," said Monty. "Pretty *loud*. That woman can *snore*. What's up with *thaaaat*?!"

Mrs. Baxter's face fell. "I do *not* snore," she whispered to her husband. "Do I?"

"No. No, baby," Mr. Baxter replied. Then he smiled. "It's more like a grunting sound." He made a noise like a hungry pig.

Mrs. Baxter was not amused.

"But," said Cory, "the most embarrassing sound my parents make is when they just ate beans—"

Afraid of what was coming next, Mr. and Mrs. Baxter both rushed onto the stage. Mr. Baxter clamped his hands over both Cory's and Monty's mouth and dragged them off the stage.

Mrs. Baxter grabbed the microphone. "Please give it up for the *farewell* performance of Cory and his buddy, Monty," she declared.

Everyone applauded.

With the early show over, Raven went back to greeting folks at the door. "Welcome to The Chill Grill. Wel—"

Raven choked on her welcome when she saw Eddie and Chelsea arrive together. "Well, well," she said coolly. "Look who's here."

Eddie was too excited about the restaurant's opening to notice that Raven was giving him attitude. "Rae, this is so tight!" he exclaimed.

"I know," Chelsea cried, looking at Raven. "Aren't you excited?"

"Excited?" said Raven. "Don't you mean hurt? Disappointed? Betrayed?"

"Oh, no, silly," said Chelsea. "The *other* excited. Like, happy."

But Eddie was starting to notice that Raven

was angry with them. "Rae," he asked, "why are you being like this?"

"Because I know what you guys were doing behind my back," Raven replied.

Chelsea and Eddie exchanged guilty looks.

"Oh, you do?" said Chelsea.

"Yeah, why didn't you tell me?" demanded Raven.

"I don't know," Chelsea replied. "We knew if we told you, you'd want to control our every move."

"I don't even want to think about y'alls moves!" Raven cried.

Eddie shot Raven a look. "Well, you're going to have to," he said. "'Cause we're going to do them onstage."

Raven was horrified. "Onstage? In front of everyone? Now, listen up, you two. My daddy runs a respectable place. You just can't get up onstage and—"

Just then, Mrs. Baxter's amplified voice announced, "Give it up for the sensational salsa dance stylings of Chelsea and Eddie!"

Raven blinked in shock. "Dance?"

Before she could say a word, Eddie and Chelsea hurried onto the stage and took their places.

Raven hurried over to her mom. "Salsa dancing?"

"Yeah, honey," Mrs. Baxter replied. "What did you think they were doing?"

"I thought they were doing something," said Raven. "But a whole different little *somethin', somethin'.*"

Raven knew she had to explain her behavior. So while Eddie and Chelsea danced the salsa, Raven stuck her big head between them. "You guys aren't going to believe this—"

Eddie and Chelsea ignored Raven and twirled across the stage. But when Chelsea went to dip Eddie, Raven had somehow reappeared.

"I thought you guys were in love with each other!" she confessed.

"What?" cried Chelsea, who was so shocked she dropped Eddie. *Thud!* He fell to the floor.

Rubbing his rear end, Eddie jumped to his feet and continued the dance. Raven trailed them around the stage.

"I had a vision that you guys were going to kiss," said Raven.

"What?" said Chelsea before Eddie led her to the other side of the stage. As they danced in front of a potted plant, Raven popped out from behind the greenery.

"I was obviously wrong," Raven admitted.

Eddie and Chelsea performed another dance move. Raven squeezed between them. "You know what?" said Raven. "Not that I would *want* to interfere or anything."

"Girl, good," barked Eddie. "Then get off the stage, Rae!"

Effortlessly, Eddie twirled Raven away. With a clear stage, Chelsea and Eddie finished their hot salsa number with a flourish. After the applause faded, Eddie and Chelsea approached Raven.

"You guys, that was so cool," Raven gushed.

"Thank you," said Chelsea.

"Thanks, Rae. And sorry we didn't tell you," said Eddie. "It's just that we wanted to do this one thing by ourselves."

"Look, *I'm* sorry, okay?" Raven replied. "For being so bossy and being in your business and thinking you two were together. And especially for that hole in the wall."

Chelsea whirled to face Raven. "What wall?"

Raven realized she said too much. "Um . . . the wall, Chelsea," stammered Raven. "You know, girl, that wall that's been blocking our friendship?"

Chelsea nodded. "That's so weird. I thought you were talking about the hole in the wall in our bathroom. We're suing the plumber."

Raven gulped. *Uh-oh*, my bad again, she thought. "Look," she said, "I just want to apologize for being so controlling this week. You know I've been so wound up with this opening and trying to make it as cool as it can be. And you know, Devon didn't even show up."

Eddie pointed to the front door. "Actually, Rae. Devon is over there, talking to your dad."

"What!" Raven couldn't believe her eyes. Devon Carter was in her dad's restaurant. Her heart pounded quickly.

"Go!" said Chelsea, pushing Raven toward Devon.

But by the time Raven crossed the room, her boy was already out the front door. "Hey, Dad, where's Devon going?!" she cried.

Mr. Baxter looked over his shoulder. "That

guy? I sent him down to Wong's. You know, you were right. Kids *do* love egg rolls."

As Mr. Baxter headed back to the kitchen, Chelsea and Eddie walked over to comfort Raven.

"Hey, you missed him, huh?" Chelsea said with a sympathetic voice.

Raven sighed. "Yeah, but, it's okay. I'd rather spend tonight with you guys." She smiled. "The Three Musketeers!"

"The Three Amigos!" Eddie cried.

"The Three Blind Mice!" Chelsea added.

Eddie and Raven stared at their clueless friend.

She got the message—and pouted. "Well, it wasn't really fair," she complained. "You guys took all the good ones."

Suddenly, the salsa music started up again.

"Ladies, shall we?" said Eddie. He held out his hands to Raven and Chelsea.

"We shall," the girls said in unison.

Then, Eddie, Chelsea, and Raven all began

to dance together. Mr. and Mrs. Baxter joined them. Soon everyone in The Chill Grill was getting their groove on!

Later that night, Mr. and Mrs. Baxter snuggled on the couch. Monty, Cory's little wooden-headed pal, was propped up next to Mrs. Baxter.

Mr. Baxter sighed with contentment. "That was like a dream come true," he said. "My own restaurant, full of family, friends, and happy customers. Thanks, babe, couldn't have done it without you. You're always there for me."

But Mrs. Baxter did not reply. When Mr. Baxter glanced over at his wife, he saw that she had fallen asleep. As she softly snored, Mr. Baxter gently covered her with a blanket.

Just then, the dummy beside Mrs. Baxter blinked its bulging eyes and said, "That's so sweet!"

For a second, Mr. Baxter stared in disbelief

at the talking dummy. Then he decided his son must have been playing a joke on him.

"That's funny, Cory," said Mr. Baxter, checking behind the couch. But Cory wasn't there.

"Cory?" Mr. Baxter called.

Cory walked in from the kitchen, eating an apple. "You call me, Dad?"

Mr. Baxter's eyes widened in shock. "Cory! But the dummy just—"

Whoa, thought Mr. Baxter, leaping off the couch. There's only one explanation for this, he thought. That block of wood is possessed!

Mrs. Baxter opened one eye and grinned at her freaked-out husband. "Gotcha!" she cried. Laughing, she pulled her hidden hand out of Monty and wiggled her fingers.

As Mr. Baxter tried to catch his breath, his wife made Monty's wooden mouth click one more time.

"What's up with *thaaaat*!?"

Part Two

Chapter One

The Chill Grill had closed for the night, but Raven and her friends were still there. Mr. Baxter had asked some friends and family to help set up for the restaurant's next big event.

Mr. Baxter set up a ladder and began to unpack decorations. While his wife searched through boxes of old clothes, Raven connected the microphones and glanced over at her homeys, Eddie and Chelsea. They didn't have much going on at the moment. That was because Cory had turned the television on. That boy will do anything to avoid work, Raven thought to herself.

Raven listened for a second when she heard the urgent tone of the anchorman's voice.

"And now the latest from Comet Watch," the announcer said.

Blah, blah, blah, Raven thought. Who cares about a stupid comet, anyway? It's not like it's something important.

The announcer continued. "Stargazers around San Francisco are eyeing the skies tonight for Pearman's Comet. The comet comes every one hundred years and is—"

Chelsea, Eddie, and Cory all groaned as the television went black. They turned to see Raven clutching the remote control.

"What are you doing?" yelled Cory. "The comet's coming!"

"Oh, it'll be back in a hundred years," said Raven. "But this weekend is *Seventies Night* and *some* of us"—Raven stared at Eddie and Chelsea meaningfully—"have to rehearse."

"And nothing says Seventies Night like a disco ball!" exclaimed Mr. Baxter. He pulled a silver, mirror-covered sphere out of a box. It sparkled in the electric blue of The Chill Grill's neon sign.

"C'mon, Eddie, give me a hand," said Mr. Baxter.

"No problem, Mr. B," Eddie replied.

Mr. Baxter handed Eddie the disco ball. Then he climbed halfway up the ladder. Eddie held the mirrored ball like a basketball.

"He shoots . . . he scores!" said Eddie, as he pretended to dunk it.

"He holds it *still*," Mr. Baxter said sternly, looking down at Eddie from the ladder.

Just then, Cory started pointing at the window and yelling, "Whoa, whoa! Look, look, it's the comet!"

Through The Chill Grill's tall windows, flashes of strange silvery light lit up the city.

"Let's go check it out!" said Cory.

Everyone followed him outside and looked

up into the night sky. The bright white comet passing over the city looked incredible.

"Ooh!" everyone gushed, like it was the Fourth of July. Everyone, that is, but Eddie.

Eddie was still holding the disco ball as he walked outside. The light from the comet struck the tiny mirrors on the ball and the dazzling display reflected in his eyes. He found the eerie glow hypnotic. He couldn't seem to look away from the ball—even when strange little lightning bolts shot from the tiny mirrors straight into his eyes.

After a few minutes of comet gazing, Raven clapped her hands. "All right, people, show's over! We've got two days to turn this place into Funky Town. C'mon!"

Everyone but Eddie headed back inside. When Eddie didn't move, Mr. Baxter grabbed the disco ball from him. Still, Eddie just stood there in a complete daze, staring into the sky.

Part One

"Get back here, Cory!" cried Raven.

"Guys! Major news," Raven squealed. "Devon Carter is going to try to come to opening night. Do you know what that means?"

"So, what's going on with you two?" asked Raven.

Eddie reached out and took Chelsea in his arms.

"Now I'm a plumber, so I'm plumbin'. 'Cause that's what plumbers do. Now get out!" Raven said.

"Hey, Monty, what did you think of my dad's oatmeal he cooked this morning?" Cory said to his dummy.

"I don't even want to think about y'alls moves!" Raven cried.

Mrs. Baxter's amplified voice announced, "Give it up for the sensational salsa dance stylings of Chelsea and Eddie!"

"What are you doing?" yelled Cory.
"The comet's coming!"

"Nothing says Seventies Night like a
disco ball!" exclaimed Mr. Baxter.

"Chels, like the way we rehearsed it, remember?
I'm supposed to say '*uh-huh*,' and you're
supposed to say '*oh, yeah*,'" Raven said.

"Now, all of a sudden I'm seeing stuff, like I'm
getting free cable inside my head," said Eddie.

"According to mine, you're getting a *kiss-off*," said Raven.

"Well, *all right!*" Eddie cried.

"'Cause we a couple of bad mama jamas
who are not diggin' the vibe you've been
puttin' down!" said Chelsea.

"Freeze, suckas!" yelled Cory. "It's party time!
Mr. Big's in town, so let's get down!"

Chelsea shook Eddie's arm. "Hey, hello?" she yelled, waving her hand. "Hello? Dude, you okay?"

At last, Eddie snapped out of it. "Yeah, great," he said with a shrug. "Let's boogie down. C'mon."

A moment later, the rehearsal began. Raven turned on the boom box. Eddie jumped onstage between Chelsea and Raven.

"Okay, ready?" Raven asked, tapping her foot. "Five, six, seven, eight . . ."

Raven shook her booty and began to sing, "'Uh-huh.'"

"'Uh-huh . . .'" echoed Chelsea.

"'Uh-huh . . .'" sang Raven.

"'Uh-huh . . .'" crooned Chelsea.

"*Uhn-unh,*" said Raven, shaking her head sadly. "Chels, like the way we rehearsed it, remember? I'm supposed to say '*uh-huh,*' and you're supposed to say '*oh, yeah.*'"

Chelsea nodded. "Oh, yeah," she said.

"See how good that sounds?" said Raven.

"Uh-huh," Chelsea replied.

Suddenly, Eddie made a face. That's weird, thought Raven. Eddie's face was all scrunched up, and one eye was closed. He seemed to be concentrating on something. Raven didn't think it was the song lyrics.

Eddie snapped out of his trance a moment later. He blinked, then noticed Raven's dad standing under the disco ball he had just hung from the ceiling.

"Mr. B, watch out!" yelled Eddie.

In a flash, Eddie jumped off the stage and tackled Mr. Baxter. A moment later, the disco ball fell where Mr. Baxter had just been standing. With a loud crash, the ball shattered into a thousand pieces.

Mr. Baxter stood up and brushed himself off. "That was close," said Mr. Baxter as he helped Eddie to his feet. "Are you okay, Eddie?"

Eddie nodded. Mr. Baxter grabbed a broom and called to his son, "Cory, help me clean this up."

Raven hurried over to her friend. "Uh, Eddie, how did you know that was going to fall?"

Eddie shrugged. "I dunno, Rae, it was kind of weird. It's like I just saw it in my head. Then it just happened."

Raven bit her lip in thought. "I think you might have had a vision," she told him.

"I did?" said Eddie, amazed. Then his face broke into a big grin. "I did!" Eddie cried, diggin' it.

Chelsea pouted. "Great! Now everybody's psychic but *me*."

Chapter Two

The next day, Eddie was still basking in the glory of saving Mr. Baxter. He relived the moment with Raven and Chelsea as they walked down the hall at school.

"You know what?" said Eddie. "I'll bet it was that comet. I mean, I was holding the disco ball and all that energy just zapped into me. Now, all of a sudden I'm seeing stuff, like I'm getting free cable inside my head."

Chelsea threw up her arms. "Great," she said. "He's psychic *and* he gets free cable. You want to rub it in a little bit more?"

Raven tried to laugh the whole thing off. "You guys, c'mon, now," she said. "One vision does not make you psychic."

Raven faced Eddie. "Besides," she added, "what was up with that goofy face you made?"

Eddie laughed along with his friends. "Oh! Oh! You mean . . ." He scrunched up his face and closed one eye. Raven was amazed he could pull off such a stupid look *twice* in a row. She and Chelsea both laughed.

But not Eddie.

When Eddie made
His wacked-out face
Through his mind
A vision raced—

Here we go again. It must be another vision. . . . Looks like Katina is in it, which is okay by me. She's one of the finest-looking girls in school. Oh, yeah!

She's carrying a big ceramic pot in her

arms. Oh, snap! It looks like a boy bumps into her. The pot flies out of Katina's arms! It's smashing against the floor and breaking into a million pieces.

"My project!" she cries. Looks like the tears are about to start falling.

The vision ended, leaving Eddie dazed and amazed. Meanwhile, Raven and Chelsea were still laughing.

"You make a face and have a vision," Raven said with a laugh. "Like it actually works like that!"

Suddenly, Eddie noticed Katina walking down the hall with a big ceramic pot in her arms. Eddie bolted, pushing past a confused Raven and Chelsea. He dropped to the ground and slid across the hall just as the boy from his vision bumped Katina.

Eddie couldn't believe what was happening.

The pot flew from Katina's hands, just like in his vision—except this time he was there to catch it and save the day.

"Got it! Got it!" said Eddie as he scrambled to his feet. "I believe this belongs to you, Katina." He handed the rescued pot back to the amazed girl.

Grinning from ear to ear, Katina hugged her precious handmade project. She tossed her blond hair over her shoulder. "Eddie, thank you," she gushed. "You totally saved my project!"

Eddie grinned. "Well . . . *you* can *save* me from being alone Saturday night."

Katina touched his arm and nodded. "Call me."

"Will do," Eddie replied.

When Eddie returned to his friends, Raven did not look happy. "Okay, uh, two things, home bro," she snapped. "One, don't *ever* use that pickup line again, in your natural born life. And two, I cannot believe you can get a vision whenever you want."

Eddie was still grinning. "I made the face. Had a vision. Got a date. It's all good!"

"Wait, Eddie," said Raven. "Do you realize what this means?"

"Yes!" Eddie replied confidently. Then he thought about the question and his face fell. "No," Eddie amended.

"It means you can't tell anybody," Raven declared.

"Right," said Eddie. Then his face fell, again. "But why not?"

"'Cause if you tell people you're psychic, they'll think you're a freak," Raven explained. "C'mon, guys, you know why I've been keeping it a secret this long?"

"All right, all right, I got you, Rae," said Eddie with a disappointed sigh. "I got to keep it on the down low."

"Right," said Raven, dropping her voice. "Keep it way, way down. Underneath stuff."

"Underneath stuff. I got you. I got you," Eddie replied, nodding.

The bell rang, and Raven and Chelsea headed off to their class. When the coast was clear, Eddie thought he'd try the whole psychic thing again. He scrunched his face and a vision began.

When Eddie made His wacked-out face Through his mind A vision raced—

Looks like I'm at The Chill Grill with my peeps. And not just Raven and Chelsea, either. I'm kickin' it with a dozen really popular kids. That's weird, I hardly know these people—but they're all acting like my friends, especially the girls! I'm the center of attention!

Sitting close beside me, Katina is giving me a look like I'm the bomb.

"Eddie, your visions are amazing," says Katina. "Everybody loves you."

And I'm just grinning and asking, "You all do? Do you all love me?"

The vision ended before Eddie got an answer. He shook his head clear and thought about what he had seen in his vision. He decided everything in it looked pretty good—especially the ladies!

"That's what I'm talking 'bout," Eddie said to himself.

He looked around and spied some of the popular kids at the end of the hall. Eddie chased after them, determined to make his vision a reality.

Chapter Three

Raven paced back and forth in the Baxters' living room, telephone in hand. She heard the busy signal—*again*—and cried, "Eddie's phone is *still* busy!"

Chelsea glanced at the clock. "Rae, it's getting late, we should just start without him."

Raven frowned. Why rehearse if a third of the band is missing? she thought. But she knew they had no choice. They were getting down to the wire. "Okay," she said with a shrug. "You're over there. Eddie's over here."

Chelsea got into position. "Okay."

Raven turned on the music, tossed her hair back, and tapped to the beat with her foot. "Five, six, seven, eight . . ." As disco music filled the Baxter house, Raven and Chelsea did a cool spin and burst into song.

"'Uh-huh,'" sang Raven.

"'Oh, yeah,'" crooned Chelsea.

Raven jumped to the middle of the chorus line, where Eddie was supposed to be. "And this is where Eddie sings. 'Uh-huh. Oh, yeah.' Eddie spins, we spin, 'Uh-huh, oh, yeah.'"

Raven jumped back to her spot. "'Uh-huh,'" she chanted.

"'Oh, yeah,'" sang Chelsea.

And Raven jumped to the middle. "And Eddie comes in again, 'Uh-huh.'"

"*Oh yeah!*" screamed Chelsea, really getting into it.

"And . . . this is not working," Raven declared.

But Chelsea kept right on groovin'. "'Oh, yeah,' not working. 'Oh, yeah, oh, yeah.' Gettin' worse—"

Raven shouted, "Chelsea!"

The still-dancing Chelsea looked over at Raven, who gestured for her friend to stop. Reluctantly, Chelsea stopped strutting.

Just then, the kitchen door swung open. Cory walked in, his chubby fingers buried deep inside a big yellow box of Cap'n Toasty's cereal.

"Hey, hey, get your grubby little hands out of there, people got to eat that stuff," said Raven.

Cory shot Raven a look that said *chill.* "I'm just digging for the prize," he explained.

Cory grinned when his fingers closed on something flat and oval shaped. He pulled it out with a big smile. "Whoa! Captain Toasty's Official Marshmallow Inspector badge."

Cory stared into the cereal box. "You're guilty, marshmallows," he declared, "of being delicious!" Cory shoved a marshmallow into his mouth, licked his fingers. Then he went for another tasty treat.

Raven yanked the cereal box out of her brother's slimy hand. "Oh, oh, no, uh-uh," Raven said, shaking her finger. "I am taking you off the case, inspector. Give me that badge."

She snapped the toy out of Cory's hand.

He was about to protest when the front door opened. Mr. and Mrs. Baxter hurried in. Mr. Baxter waved a videocassette in the air. He couldn't hide the excitement in his voice.

"Look what I scored at the video store. *Undercover Disco Divas,*" Mr. Baxter cried.

Mrs. Baxter nodded enthusiastically. "This should help get us ready for Seventies Night."

Mr. Baxter shoved the cassette into the machine, then turned on the television.

"Yeah!" Mr. Baxter declared. "Lay some eyeballs on *this* hip classic flick."

Then Mr. Baxter spun around the living room, gathering everyone around the television. When they were all seated, Mr. Baxter flopped onto the couch and pressed PLAY.

The first thing Raven saw on the TV screen was a tiny apartment with too many curtains and a black velvet picture on the wall.

Can you say tacky? she thought to herself.

Then she heard the throb of disco music in the background as two dudes in velvet suits and platform shoes sat in big chairs, counting dollar bills. They had bushy Afro haircuts and wore thick chains around their necks.

What color is that rug? Raven wondered with a frown. Whatever it is, it's nasty!

Suddenly, the door flew open and two female cops burst in. Raven's eyes widened at the '70s stylin' going on. They wore big, bushy Afro wigs, crazy jumpsuits that were neon blue and orange, and platform shoes so high the women looked like they were walking on stilts!

"Freeze, suckas!" yelled the woman with the brown 'fro. They both whipped out their badges.

"Dang!" cursed one of the bad guys. "It's the Undercover Disco Divas!"

"Sho' 'nuff, sugar," said the cop with the big brown Afro. "I'm Coffee."

The cop with the white Afro stepped forward. "And I'm Cream," she declared, striking a pose.

"And you two jive turkey bank robbers are stone-cold busted!" Coffee announced.

Cream nodded. "'Cause we're a couple of bad mama jamas, and we ain't diggin' the vibe you be putting down."

The bad guys jumped out of their chairs. They weren't going down without a fight.

"Ain't no foxy mamas going to stop our groove," said the dude with the big chain around his neck. "Get 'em!"

The bad guys charged, but the ladies just grooved out of the way. The dudes ran into one another and fell to the ground. The Undercover Disco Divas finished them off with a few dance steps and a couple of chop-socky moves.

"Oh, man," moaned the lead bad guy. "We got discoed down."

Coffee dusted her hands off. "That'll teach them to mess around with the foxiest fuzz."

Coffee and Cream slapped hands.

"Right on, my sister," said Cream. They both flashed peace signs and struck a pose, and the shot froze. Then the main titles spun out of the screen in big psychedelic letters that spelled out: UNDERCOVER DISCO DIVAS.

"This is so cool!" Cory declared. "Where has *this* been all my life?"

Everybody shushed Cory. Their eyes were still glued to the television screen.

Chapter Four

"**S**o, did you hear from Eddie?" Chelsea asked Raven the next morning at school.

"No!" said Raven. "And I called his house like, a zillion times." Raven rolled her eyes. "And I think his mom's starting to get a little attitudinal problem or something."

They saw Eddie in the hall a moment later. He was hanging with Katina. Raven and Chelsea hurried to greet their best friend, but they weren't fast enough. A group of admirers got there first, cutting in front of Raven and pushing Chelsea aside.

Then Katina blocked everyone—including Raven and Chelsea. "Okay, okay, people," Katina cried. "Look. Eddie can only tell *one* future at a time." She whirled to face him. "Me first!" she demanded.

"Okay." Eddie took a deep breath and twisted his face.

Raven just shook her head. "There he goes making that *vision* face. What *is* that?"

When Eddie snapped out of his trance, he patted Katina on the back. "Congratulations, girl," he told her, "you're getting a B in bio."

Katina smiled with pride, and Eddie grinned.

"Move over here, excuse me, now," Eddie said, pushing through the crowd.

Eddie stood behind a couple who were holding hands. He placed an arm on each of their shoulders. As he made his psychic face, images appeared in his head. Then he looked at the girl. "Uh, you're going to the prom," he told her, "but not with him."

She gasped and dropped the boy's hand.

"Sorry," said Eddie, who was already moving on.

Raven and Chelsea finally caught up with their friend a few predictions later.

"Hey, what's up, Eddie, how you doin'?" said Raven. Then she tugged on his arm. "Can I speak to you for a second?"

Eddie shook his head. "Rae, actually, I'm with my people here," he said.

Raven waved at the crowd and smiled through gritted teeth. "Oh, what's up, people? What's up?"

Then Raven grabbed Eddie by the arm. "Get your little psychic butt over here," she hissed.

Eddie stood his ground. "Rae—"

"Get it over here," Raven commanded.

Eddie rolled his eyes. "What in the world?"

"Where were you last night?" Raven asked as Chelsea looked on.

Eddie slapped his forehead. "That's right, the song. Well, you know, I was a little busy, you know, making predictions and stuff."

Raven frowned. "Eddie, I thought you said you weren't going to tell anybody."

"What is the big deal, Rae?" Eddie asked, throwing up his hands. "I mean, they have questions and I have answers. I'm just trying to keep everyone happy. Especially the *cute* ones."

Eddie winked and blew Katina a kiss. She smiled sweetly, pretending to catch it.

Raven and Chelsea both pretended to gag.

"I'll see you at lunch, Edward," Katina called.

"Okay," Eddie cooed in reply.

Suddenly, Raven froze and her eyes glazed over. Eddie stepped back.

"She's having a vision," Chelsea said with a sigh. Feeling left out, she began to file her nails.

"Oh, yeah?" cried Eddie. "Well, *two* can

play the psychic game, you know?" Then he made his vision face.

Chelsea threw up her hands. "Oh, great," she groaned. "*Now* there's a *game* I can't play."

Through her eye
The vision runs
Flash of future
Here it comes—

Okay, vision, bring it on!

Looks like I'm watching Eddie and Katina in the hall in front of Eddie's locker. They're acting pretty sweet on each other, like they're an item or something.

Whoa, what's this? Katina is giving Eddie attitude and making him talk to the hand!

Poor Eddie looks really crushed. Now Katina is turning her back on him and strutting away.

Meanwhile, Eddie was having a vision of his own. . . .

When Eddie made
His wacked-out face
Through his mind
A vision raced—

I'm in the hall, looking good . . . and here comes Katina. She is so fine! And she's giving me the look that says I got it all.

Now she's tossing her long, blond hair. She's leaning close and kissing me! All right! I like this vision thing.

The vision left as quickly as it had come. A grin spread across Eddie's face. But Raven didn't see it. She was lost in her own vision.

When both Raven and Eddie came out of

their trances, they found Chelsea, totally bored and annoyed, still filing her nails.

"So, how's the future?" she asked with attitude. "Not like *I* would know or anything."

Raven sadly shook her head. "Eddie, you and Katina . . . it's not looking good."

Eddie couldn't believe what he was hearing. He decided to set Raven straight. "According to *my* vision, I'm getting a kiss."

Raven shook her head. "According to mine, you're getting a *kiss-off*."

"You're just jealous," Eddie shot back.

"Of what?" Raven asked.

Eddie thrust his thumb in his chest. "Of how popular I am, Rae."

"Popular?" Raven cried. Now it was her turn to set him straight. "Eddie, you actually think those people are your friends? They're just using you to get your predictions!"

Eddie was really getting tired of being dogged by Raven. "Oh, yeah?" he told her. "Well, here's another prediction. I'm out of here!"

Angrily, Eddie turned his back on Raven and Chelsea and walked away.

"Well, come on," said Chelsea. "Even I could have predicted *that*."

Chapter Five

That night, The Chill Grill was jammin'. The place was packed, and everyone was having fun, except Raven and Chelsea. They sat at a table in glum silence, staring off into space.

Mr. Baxter arrived at the Table of Doom with a plate of his delicious, hand-cut fries and ice-cold bottles of water.

"So," said Mr. Baxter, "you guys still not talking to Eddie?"

Raven nodded. "Ever since he became psychic, he thinks he's all that."

"Oh, come on," said Mr. Baxter. "Eddie? He's still the same old, humble guy."

A crowd of kids from Bayside, led by Katina, stampeded into the restaurant, carrying Eddie on their shoulders. They cheered and hooted. Eddie grinned and waved to the crowd.

"Eddie! Eddie!" they chanted.

Eddie threw out his arms. "I'm king of the world!" he bellowed. The chanting swelled until it filled the dining room. "Eddie, Eddie, Eddie . . ."

They lowered Eddie to the ground and made room for him at the center of a huge table.

From across the room, Raven and Chelsea watched their former friend with his new homeys.

"See?" said Mr. Baxter. "The same old, humble king of the world."

Mr. Baxter headed for the kitchen. The gang around Eddie clamored for predictions of their future.

"Eddie, you were right," gushed Katina. "I got a B on my bio test!"

Everyone cheered. If Eddie was right about

Katina's grade, that meant his predictions did come true. Eddie slipped his arm around Katina and pulled her close, reveling in the moment.

"Your visions are amazing," Katina declared. "Everybody loves you."

Eddie's grin lit up the room. "You all do? You all love me?"

Across the room, Chelsea put down her french fry. "You know what, Rae? I was thinking," she began. "You know how you never wanted anyone knowing you were psychic, 'cause you thought they'd all think you were, like, a freak or something?"

Raven nodded. "Yeah?"

"Well, I dunno," Chelsea continued. "Maybe you should *tell* them. I mean, look at Eddie. Apparently, people like freaks."

Raven opened her mouth to reply, but she was interrupted by cheers from across the room.

At Eddie's table, Katina addressed the

crowd. "You know what I'm talking about," she said. "Who thinks Eddie should have his own TV show?"

Eddie seemed surprised by the question. "I mean, would you all watch that?" he asked.

Everyone cheered in reply, shouting they'd watch every single day.

Raven rolled her eyes. "Okay, now that's just ridiculous. I mean, *who* would watch a show about a teen psychic?"

Chelsea shrugged.

At the other table, Eddie excused himself to go to the restroom. On his way back, an older teen who was wearing a velour tracksuit with a thick gold chain around his neck stepped in front of Eddie.

He slipped a toothpick between his teeth and offered Eddie his hand. "Hey, Eddie. Sonny Curtis, remember me? I went to your school last year."

Eddie shook the older boy's hand. He's a big dude, Eddie thought to himself. He had to crane his neck just to look Sonny in the eye. "Sonny! What's poppin' with you, man?"

Sonny shrugged. "Nothin, really. I hear you're pretty good at making predictions."

"Yeah," Eddie said with a smug smile. "It's a gift."

"Word is, you're on a hot streak," said Sonny.

Eddie nodded and puffed up his chest proudly. "Haven't been wrong yet."

"Well, let's try a little experiment, huh?" said Sonny. He reached into his pocket, pulled out a notebook, and handed it to Eddie.

"Take a look at these names," said Sonny. "Anything pop out at you?"

Eddie took the pages and touched his head. "Well, let's see what I can whip up, you know?"

Eddie scanned the list and did his thing. . . .

When Eddie made
His wacked-out face
Through his mind
A vision raced—

Check it out . . . I'm seeing nothing but a scoreboard. It's a big one, too. But it's completely empty. No! Scratch that. The lights are coming on, so bright they're blinding me. I can't read it.

Wait, I see it now! Two words are flashing on the board in big, bold letters: LIVE WIRE.

Eddie snapped back to reality. He didn't understand what his vision had meant. But he told Sonny, anyway. "I saw the name Live Wire. That mean anything?"

Sonny grinned and wiggled the toothpick in his mouth. "We'll find out," he said. Then he reached into his pocket and slipped a crinkled bill into Eddie's palm.

Eddie was shocked. "Yo, Sonny! This is twenty bones!"

"Man," Sonny replied, "if you're as good as you say you are, there's a lot more where that came from."

"Well, all right, Sonny!" Eddie called. *Dang,* he thought, grinning at the twenty-dollar bill. *It looks like this vision thing is paying off in more ways than one!* Then he slipped the money into his pocket and went back to his table of admirers.

When Cory got home from school, his dad was in the kitchen. His mother was talking on the telephone.

"He said what?!" Mrs. Baxter cried. She shook her head, looking very concerned. Then Mrs. Baxter spotted Cory lurking in the doorway and shot him a stern look.

"Oh, don't worry," said Mrs. Baxter. "My

husband and I are going to have a serious talk with *Cory* about this."

Cory heard his name and did a quick about-face, but it wasn't quick enough. His father snagged him by the collar before he could escape.

"Hold up there, cool breeze!" Mr. Baxter warned his son.

Mrs. Baxter hung up the telephone. She whirled to face her son. "Cory," she snapped, "did you call your teacher a jive-turkey sucker?"

Cory's father couldn't believe what he was hearing. But Cory grinned proudly. "Somebody had to stand up to *The Man*," he told his parents.

Mrs. Baxter frowned at her son. "Mrs. Applebaum is not *The Man*. Cory, how many times did you watch that *Disco Divas* tape your father brought home?"

"Just a dozen, cousin," Cory replied, using the '70s slang again. He crossed the kitchen and sat down at the table.

With a sigh of disappointment, Mr. Baxter faced his son. "Cory, just because people act a certain way in the movies doesn't mean they act that way in real life."

Cory's mother nodded in agreement. "Honey, when you go to school tomorrow you have to apologize to Mrs. Applebaum."

Cory frowned. "And the lunch lady, too?" he asked.

Mrs. Baxter's eyebrows rose. "What did you say to her?" she asked.

Cory grinned. "I told her without the hair-net she'd look like one foxy mama!"

Chapter Six

At school the next day, Eddie was headed for his locker when Katina caught up with him.

"Hey, Eddie," she called.

"Hey," said Eddie, pleased to see her.

Katina leaned close and gave Eddie a kiss.

"Just like my vision," he said. I *knew* Raven's vision was wrong, he thought triumphantly.

"Oh, you're so sweet," Katina replied. "Now, make that cute little face and tell me if I'm going to be captain of the cheerleaders!"

Eddie gave her the thumbs-up. "You got it, baby. Let me see what I can do."

Eddie put his index finger to his forehead. He scrunched up his features.

But nothing came.

Eddie tried again. This time he squinted a little harder. Once again, his mind came up blank. Eddie's psychic powers had failed him.

"What's wrong, Eddie?" Katina demanded impatiently.

"Uh, uh, nothin'. Nothin'," Eddie stammered. He tried to concentrate. "Let me see . . ."

But Eddie came up blank again. He saw nothing. He heard nothing—except Katina's angry voice. Where was the vision?

"Is there a problem?" she asked.

"No!" Eddie cried. "I just got a lot on my mind. This never happened to me before."

Katina put her hands on her hips. "Okay, so you're saying you can't come up with anything?" she asked.

"Woman, I'm trying!" Eddie snapped. "If you would stop putting so much pressure on me—"

"Well, if you can't tell me the future, we *have* no future," Katina declared.

Eddie watched in complete disbelief as Katina gave him her hand—just like Raven warned him she would!

Shaken, Eddie watched Katina go. "Whatever," he called after her.

Eddie was still dazed as he opened his locker. Suddenly, he heard throbbing music. He peeked in his locker and saw a boom box with speakers. Eddie slammed the door.

I must have opened the wrong locker, he thought. Eddie checked the number on the door. It was his, all right. He opened his locker again, and the boom box started up once again. It filled the hallway with a thumping bass beat.

Eddie took a closer look and couldn't believe his eyes. His locker had been decked out with a velvet lining, flashing lights, and an expensive stereo system.

"Well, *all right*!" Eddie cried as he danced to the beat.

A hand reached out and closed the locker. When the music stopped, Eddie turned to find Sonny grinning at him. The older boy was wearing even more gold chains than before, and his brand-new track shoes were totally fly.

"You like the way I hooked you up?" Sonny asked.

Eddie pumped Sonny's hand. "Man, Sonny, you did this, man? That's funky, man. But why?"

Sonny patted Eddie on the back. "That horse you picked *won*."

Eddie's mouth gaped in surprise. "What horse?" he asked.

"*Live Wire*," said Sonny. "He won the race, and I won a bundle."

"Wait a minute," Eddie said. He was just

beginning to understand why Sonny was being so nice to him. "I picked a horse for you to bet on? Man, that's gambling, dawg."

Sonny grinned and stuck a toothpick between his teeth. "Not when it's a sure thing."

"Yeah, I guess so," Eddie said, but he wasn't too happy about being used.

Sonny reached into his back pocket. He pulled out the betting sheets for the day's horse races. "Now," said Sonny. "I need you to do that thing you do and pick me out a winner." Sonny thrust the paper into Eddie's hand.

Reluctantly, Eddie looked over the names. "Man, I don't know," he said after a long pause.

Sonny's friendly smile vanished. His eyes narrowed and his voice became threatening. "Man, look, just make that stupid face and tell me who's going to win!"

"Right," said Eddie nervously. The big guy was obviously angry. And Eddie sure didn't want to make him any angrier.

Placing his finger to his head, he squinted and made his crazy vision face. He tried as hard as he could, but he just wasn't getting anything. Finally, Eddie opened one eye to see if Sonny was still watching.

He was.

Eddie closed his eyes again and tried even harder. "Sonny . . . I'm getting something," Eddie said at last. Eddie ran his finger down the list of names. Then he picked one at random, taking a shot just to get rid of Sonny.

"Murr the Blur," Eddie declared.

Sonny blinked, surprised. "Murr the Blur?"

"Murr the Blur," said Eddie, trying to sound confident.

"Interesting," said Sonny, checking the racing sheet. "Murr the Blur's never won a race before. He's going to pay off big-time." Before heading off to place his bet, he warned Eddie. "I'm betting it *all* on this one."

"Yeah," groaned Eddie. "I guess *I* am, too."

Seventies Night was just hours away. Raven and Chelsea were rehearsing their disco act—sans Eddie. Their retro costumes hung on racks behind them.

As she sat on the couch, Raven combed out her huge blond Afro wig. Chelsea sat beside her friend, combing out her brown Afro wig.

"I don't know, Rae," sighed Chelsea. "I still wish Eddie was doing the song with us tonight."

Raven shook her head. "Unh-unh, Chels. I thought we said we're *not* going to talk about him."

"You're right," Chelsea cried. "I forgot. Not a word."

"Right," said Raven. "Because, you know, he decided to ditch us." She began picking at the wig violently, yanking the bushy locks with ferocity. "And, yeah. It may seem great. I mean, he's all popular now. And all the girls are like, 'Oh, Eddie, you're so cute. You're so psychic, Eddie.'"

Raven went from picking the wig to *stabbing* it with her comb, again and again! "'Oh, Eddie,'" Raven continued. "'You got the greatest little eyes—'"

Chelsea dropped her comb and grabbed Raven's arm. "Rae, Rae, Rae, calm down! Come on, now, don't wig out." Chelsea froze for a second, then burst into laughter. "Get it?" she cried. "Like *wig out.*"

While Chelsea chuckled at her own lame joke, Raven felt a familiar tingle. Another vision was coming on.

Through her eye
The vision runs
Flash of future
Here it comes—

Whoa, where am I? Looks like The Chill Grill. I hear the disco beat, it must be tonight—Seventies Night.

Oh, no. That big dude Sonny is grabbing Eddie by the collar and getting in his face. Eddie is really sweating and not from the heat.

"Look," Eddie's pleading. "Just be easy, okay?"

Now I'm seeing that big watch on Sonny's arm—it says seven o'clock!

Raven blinked as she came out of her vision.

"*Omigosh,* Chelsea!" Raven gasped. "I just had a vision. Eddie's going to be in trouble. He's at The Chill Grill. We've got to help him!"

Chapter Seven

The Chill Grill wasn't open yet. But it was totally decked out for Seventies Night. A big, mirrored disco ball dangled from the ceiling. Disco tunes filled the air. And lava lamps of every color bubbled and rolled on the dining room tables.

Mr. Baxter was grooving behind the counter while he loaded up silverware trays. On his head, a massive Afro wig bobbed up and down to the disco beat. The music was so loud, Mr. Baxter couldn't hear the phone ringing. He couldn't have known that Raven was trying to warn him that Eddie was in trouble—or soon would be.

As he danced, Mr. Baxter looked up to see

Eddie walking in. His hands were in his pockets, and his face looked tense. He shifted back and forth nervously. Mr. Baxter turned off the music.

Eddie waved. "Hey, what's up, Mr. B?"

"Hey, hey, hey!" Mr. Baxter cried with a grin. He tried to cheer up Eddie by bobbing his Afro.

"Mind if I hang out?" Eddie asked. "Watch a little TV. News, sports, *horse race results?*"

"Oh, yeah, sure," Mr. Baxter replied. He figured Eddie had probably just had a bad day at school and needed to chill. So he tossed him the television remote. "Make yourself at home. You know, Seventies Night's about to start in about an hour. I need to go home and get my boogie clothes on."

"Wait, wait, Mr. B," Eddie cried. "You're not going to leave me here alone, are you?"

Mr. Baxter nodded, his crazy wig dropping

over his eyes. "Oh, yeah, sure, you stay here, keep an eye on the place. That way I don't have to lock up."

Then Mr. Baxter was out the door, leaving a worried Eddie behind. Wringing his hands, Eddie crossed the room and sank into a chair. He looked up at the TV screen.

"*Dang*. Okay, TV," Eddie said, switching it on.

The local news had just come back from a commercial break. "Here is the latest from Comet Watch," said the anchorman.

Eddie sat up straighter in his chair.

"Pearman's Comet has left the building," the anchor continued. "Good-bye for another hundred years. And good-bye to all those wacky stories of people claiming the comet gave them weird powers!"

Eddie buried his face in his hands. "Boy," he moaned. "There's a lot of nuts out there."

"And now, a sports update," said the anchorman. "A new record was just set as Murr the Blur came in dead last for the twenty-seventh time."

Eddie listened to the news in horror. Then he turned off the television with a moan. He laid his aching head down on the table and closed his eyes. When he opened them again, a shadow had fallen over him.

"Some race, huh?" said Sonny.

Eddie looked up. "Sonny, my man—"

Sonny stepped closer. Eddie gulped. The dude had always been tall. But this close, and this angry, he somehow seemed even taller.

"I was counting on you, man," Sonny said tightly. "What happened?"

Eddie forced a shrug. He tried to show Sonny that they should just laugh the whole thing off. "Well, you know that comet that came through the other day? Funny thing—"

Unfortunately, Sonny wasn't in the mood to laugh. "There's nothing *funny* about me losing my money, see. 'Cause when I lose, *you* pay."

"Yeah, guy," said Eddie. "But if we were in an opposite universe—then I would lose, and you would pay. . . . Okay, that's still not good."

Sonny grabbed Eddie by his shirt and hauled him off his feet. "Look, just be easy, okay?" Eddie pleaded.

Suddenly, the front door burst open.

"Freeze suckas!" Raven and Chelsea cried as they strutted into the restaurant.

Both girls were totally decked out in their '70s threads. They wore big Afro wigs and bell-bottom pants. Raven's wig was milk white. Her lips were a frosty pink, the perfect complement to her pink-and-red psychedelic shirt, chocolate brown jumpsuit, and red platform shoes. Chelsea wore a brown Afro.

Her pantsuit was lemon yellow, and her platform shoes were shiny white.

Both girls flashed shiny silver badges, then threw out a couple of kung fu kicks. Raven almost fell off her platforms, then quickly regained her balance.

"What's going on?" demanded Sonny. "Who are you two?"

Raven stepped forward, tottering on her stacked shoes. "I'm Coffee," she declared.

Chelsea threw her head back, and her Afro wig bobbed. "And I'm Cream."

"And *you* are stone-cold busted," said Raven, shaking a finger at Sonny.

Sonny seemed skeptical. "You're cops?"

"Yeah, I know these two, man," said Eddie, playing along. "You in trouble now, Sonny-boy."

"Sho' 'nuff," Chelsea chirped, remembering all that *Undercover Disco Divas* slang from Mr.

Baxter's favorite '70s movie. "'Cause we a couple of bad mama jamas who are not diggin' the vibe you've been puttin' down!"

Sonny blinked, then scratched his head. "What does that mean?" he asked.

"It means if you stop putting the squeeze on my little soul brother over there," said Raven, "we're gonna forget this ever happened. Ya dig? Ya dig? Ya dig?"

"Wait a second," Sonny cried. "What kind of cops are you?" He stepped forward, snatched Chelsea's badge, and read it. "'Captain Toasty's Official Marshmallow Inspector'?!"

"Hey, it's a tough job, okay?" Chelsea cried defensively. "You ever try handcuffing a marshmallow? It's really hard, and they get really sticky, and the ring around the marshmallow gets so messed up—"

Raven cringed. *Yikes*, she thought, *somebody's*

taking her cop role just a little too *seriously*!
"Cream, Cream, Cream," said Raven, calming
her hysterical friend. "I'll handle it."

Raven whirled and faced Sonny. "We're two
foxy mamas you just don't want to mess with."
She threw a few more karate kicks.

"Man, knock it off!" Sonny cried, clearly
not buying the whole kung fu groove thing.
"There's no way you two are cops."

"Are totally," Chelsea argued.

"Enough," Sonny roared. "You guys are
going down." Sonny lurched toward Raven,
who dropped back into a fighting crouch.

That's when Eddie intervened. He jumped
between Sonny and his two best friends.
"Wait, hold up!" he told Sonny. "Look, man, I
picked the horse, and you bet it. *They* had
nothing to do with it."

"You're right," Sonny replied. "And *you're*
going down!"

Once again, Sonny grabbed Eddie by his shirt. Eddie closed his eyes, preparing for the worst. That's when Mr. and Mrs. Baxter burst through the front door.

Wearing their '70s clothes, they were totally clueless about what was going on. They just thought it would be funny to burst into the room like the stars of their favorite old flick.

"Freeze, suckas!" bellowed Mr. Baxter.

"Put your hands in the air!" yelled Mrs. Baxter.

Sonny bought the act. He let go of Eddie and threw up his hands.

Then Raven's mother threw up her own hands. "And wave them like you just don't care. Hey!" she sang.

Mr. and Mrs. Baxter started doing a disco dance, and Sonny looked totally confused. "What's going on?!" he demanded.

"It's Seventies Night," said Mr. Baxter. "Where are your threads?"

"Wait a minute," said Mrs. Baxter. "Aren't you Gloria and George's little boy, *Sanford*?"

Sonny stood tall, adjusting his tracksuit. "I'm *Sonny*, now."

"Well, *Sonny-now*," said Mr. Baxter, "what have you been up to?"

"I'll tell you, Dad," said Raven. "A little gambling . . . and threatening Eddie. A little of *that*."

Sonny loomed over Raven and hissed, "This is none of your business."

Mr. Baxter was about to straighten the kid out when Mrs. Baxter pushed him aside. "Oh, it's going to be *your mother's* business when I call her," she warned him.

"Oh, come on," Sonny said. "You're not really going to call my mom."

Mrs. Baxter put her hand out. "Mr. Baxter, your phone, please?"

Mr. Baxter's hands dug around his huge Afro. He pulled out a cell phone and handed it to his wife.

Sonny looked stricken. "Oh, come on, please don't tell my mom." Suddenly, the big tough guy started whining like a little kid. "I'll be grounded for a year. Come on!"

But Mrs. Baxter was already flipping the telephone open. With a scared little squeal, Sonny ran out of the restaurant and into the night.

Eddie shook his head. "And I was afraid of that guy?"

Mrs. Baxter went to the door and shouted, "You can run, but I'm *still* calling your mother, Sanford!"

Inside the restaurant, Mr. Baxter turned to Eddie, Raven, and Chelsea. "So, uh, you guys okay?"

Raven nodded, hugged her father. "Yeah, Dad, we're cool. Thanks."

Eddie shook Mr. Baxter's hand. "Good lookin' out, Mr. B," he said. Then he gestured to Raven and Chelsea. "You mind giving us a minute? That is, if these guys are still talking to me."

Mr. Baxter smiled and eased back into his '70s character. "You got it, brotha man."

But Raven and Chelsea were still angry. They turned their backs on Eddie and started walking away.

"Wait, wait, Rae, Chels!" Eddie called. "How did you know I was in trouble?"

Raven shot him a look. "I had a vision," she said. "I mean, unlike you, I can't get them anytime I want to. But when I do, they come in handy, don't they?"

Eddie nodded. "Well, mine are gone, and I'm actually pretty glad. Because this whole psychic thing is just way more complicated than I thought, you know, Rae?"

Chelsea rolled her eyes. "Well, you know, she tried to tell you!"

"Eddie, listen, okay," said Raven. "I have been going though this my entire life, and I still don't know how they work."

Eddie leaned against a counter. "So, uh, are we still friends?" he asked.

Raven eyed him. "That depends. I mean, can you get down and funky?" She began to strut around, showing him her disco moves. Chelsea joined in.

"Sho' 'nuff, my sistahs," said Eddie, getting down with his chicks.

Suddenly, the front door to The Chill Grill opened and Cory walked in. He wore a sky blue tuxedo and a long, blue-feathered coat. On his head, a huge matching blue fedora topped a massive Afro, and around his neck hung a chain with a big silver dollar sign.

"Freeze, suckas!" yelled Cory. "It's party

time! Mr. Big's in town, so let's get down!"

In the kitchen, Mr. Baxter threw the switch and the party started. Disco music filled the restaurant, the lights went low, and the lava lamps glowed on the tables with psychedelic style.

The partygoers arrived in a flood. They were all in Seventies Night costumes. And everyone started groovin' to the funky-town sound.

Later that night, when The Chill Grill was really kickin', Mrs. Baxter jumped onto the stage. "Brothers and sisters," she announced into the microphone. "Let's give a funky Seventies Night welcome to Eddie 'Brotha-man' Thomas and his Foxy Ladies!"

The crowd exploded in applause as Raven, Chelsea, and Eddie took the stage. The music swelled as the song "Disco Dude" blasted out of the speakers.

"*Uh-huh,*" sang Raven.

"*Oh, yeah,*" crooned Chelsea.

"*Uh-huh,*" belted Raven.

"*Oh, yeah,*" yelled Chelsea.

Then out came Eddie. "I'm a real funky dude," he sang. "In a crazy disco mood. I'm one bad brother who dances like a—"

"'Shut your mouth!'" sang Raven and Chelsea.

"'Ain't going to take no jive, 'cause I'm feeling so alive,'" crooned Eddie. "'Let's boogie down and shake it all around.'"

"'He's a Disco Dude in a crazy funky mood,'" sang Raven and Chelsea. "'He's lookin' so hot and he just can't stop.'"

"'Oh, yeah!'" yelled Eddie with a kick and a spin.

The song worked its magic. The crowd got into it and was ready to disco the night away.

Raven couldn't have been any happier.

Everything was back to normal. She was back to being the only one with visions of the future, even when they involved a blast from the past like Seventies Night. But best of all, she and Eddie and Chelsea were friends again.

Coffee, Cream, and Brotha-man Eddie— back together again. That's what I'm talkin' about, Raven thought to herself as she danced with her homeys.

Gaze into the future and take a sneak peek at the next *That's So Raven* story. . . .

Adapted by Alice Alfonsi

Based on the television series, "That's So Raven", created by Michael Poryes and Susan Sherman

Based on the episode written by Ed Evans

This is messed up, thought Eddie Thomas. The first bell hadn't even rung yet and Principal Lawler was already acting freaky.

"The nose knows," Lawler muttered to himself. The stocky, gray-haired man moved down the hall, smelling students' lockers. *Sniff, sniff, sniff*. . .

Eddie shook his head. Lawler hasn't been principal very long, he thought. Maybe the pressure is getting to him.

Standing beside Eddie, Chelsea Daniels flipped back her long, red hair. She didn't care what Lawler's problem was. The man was about to invade her *aromatic* privacy, and she was going to say something about it!

"Principal Lawler," she snapped, storming right up to him, "is someone being a little bit *nosy*?"

Lawler straightened up. "P-p-pipe down, Miss Daniels," he ordered, staring at Chelsea through his partially crossed eyes. "I am p-p-pretty p-perturbed!"

Chelsea recoiled as Lawler's spit-storm of

sputtering *P*'s drenched her with saliva. *Eeeww*, she thought, that is just *gross*!

Hanging back, Eddie tried not to laugh at Chelsea's mistake. She'd forgotten the First Rule of Lawler. Never stand closer than two feet from the man. His geyser of spit was as dependable as Old Faithful!

Eddie had learned this from personal experience. Back when Lawler was still teaching English, Eddie had been forced to sit in the front row. He'd silently chanted *rain, rain, go away* for an entire semester. It hadn't helped. The spray had gotten so bad, he'd pulled garbage bags over his clothes just to keep them dry.

"The Gourmet Cooking Club is missing a very expensive, very p-p-pungent P-P-Parmesan," Lawler continued, "and I intend to *sniff* it out."

Eddie wasn't sure he'd heard right. "You mean

to tell me someone jacked some *stanky* cheese?"

"P-p-precisely!" Lawler replied, spraying Chelsea like a lawn sprinkler.

"Oh, man," she whispered to Eddie as she wiped her face, "you had to ask. Why?"

"Things need to tighten up around here," Lawler declared angrily. "P-p-people come to school like it's one big p-p-party."

Chelsea was about to argue that point when her best friend, Raven Baxter, burst through the double doors at the end of the hall. "Party over here! Party over here!" Raven sang to the music blasting in her headphones.

Mr. Lawler didn't notice Raven right away. He had gone back to sniffing lockers. Unfortunately, Raven didn't notice Mr. Lawler, either. She kept bustin' moves down the hall, wildly swinging her arms, causing the huge lilac ruffles on her sleeves to sail through the air.

"Party over here! Party over here!" Raven

continued to sing at the top of her lungs. She twirled three times. The matching ruffles she'd sewn into her bell-bottoms spun with her.

Chelsea and Eddie waved their hands and pointed to Lawler, who was just a few feet away, sniffing lockers. But Raven didn't notice the principal. She just waved her hands and pointed, too, imitating her friends. She figured they were doing some old steps.

"Jump, jump!" she cried, still grooving to the music. "Hey, that's old school. Jump, jump!"

Finally, Mr. Lawler turned and saw Raven.

And *she* finally saw *him*.